MW00917619

THE MURDER AT THE INN

AN ABIGAIL LAPP AMISH MYSTERY

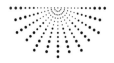

ESTHER RABER

PURE READ

Publisher's Note: This is a work of fiction. Names, characters, places, and incidents are a product of the author's imagination. Locales and public names are sometimes used for atmospheric purposes. Any resemblance to actual people, living or dead, or to businesses, companies, events, institutions, or locales is completely coincidental.

© 2018 PUREREAD LTD

CONTENTS

A Personal Word From PureRead   v

Chapter 1   1
Chapter 2   7
Chapter 3   12
Chapter 4   20
Chapter 5   27
Chapter 6   39
Chapter 7   46
Chapter 8   55
Chapter 9   62
Chapter 10   67
About PureRead   72

Boxset Reading Enjoyment   75
PureRead Reader Club   77

A PERSONAL WORD FROM PUREREAD

 Dear reader,

It is our utmost pleasure and privilege to bring these wonderful stories to you. I am so very proud of our amazing team of Christian writers, and the delight they continually bring to us all with their beautiful tales of hope, faith, courage and love.

Only once a story is read does it fulfil it's God given purpose, and that makes you, the dear reader, the key that unlocks the treasures that lay within the pages of this book.

Thank you for choosing PureRead!

A PERSONAL WORD FROM PUREREAD

THANK YOU FOR CHOOSING PUREREAD. WHY NOT
SIGN UP FOR UPDATES AND BECOME PART OF OUR
EXCLUSIVE READER CLUB (IT'S FREE TO JOIN)

 JOIN THE READER CLUB (IT'S FREE)

**To sign up for PureRead Updates Go To
Pureread.com/readerclub**

CHAPTER ONE

Abigail Lapp stood on the very top of the stepladder, reaching as high as her short stature would allow to hang a bough of garland. She had nearly finished decorating for Christmastime. The greeting cards from her friends and neighbors had been displayed on the mantel, surrounded by a length of greenery. Abigail had carefully wrapped each of the presents she had made and set them near the hearth. She looked forward to seeing the eager faces of her loved ones as they opened their scarves, hats, dolls, and books. The Troyer Farms Bed and Breakfast was coming together for the season, and Abigail looked forward to spending time with her family and honoring Christ.

There was no place that Abigail enjoyed more than being at the Inn. Formerly one of the farmhouses, the building's numerous rooms and proximity to the road that led into the small Amish village of Mount Hope made it an ideal location for a bed and breakfast. Her great-grandfather had built the stone house with the help of his brothers and sons, and the place still stood solidly. Abigail had always enjoyed the beauty of the *haus* even as a child, and it warmed her heart to know that she could put it to such good use even though the family didn't live in it anymore. Her guests enjoyed the long covered porch that ran down the entire front of the house and wrapped around one side. There were no modern amenities here that her fellow Amish wouldn't approve of. The locals appreciated it, and even her *Englisch* guests seemed to enjoy a change of pace from their busy lives.

There was something particularly special for Abigail in running a bed and breakfast. She had been a happy housewife once, spending her time in the garden during the summer and over the stove during the winter. Though she and her husband had not been blessed with children, Abigail had still managed to fill her days with cooking, quilting, sewing, and cleaning. If she found that she had spare time on her hands, she walked to the barn and assisted her family members on the dairy farm.

This left her exhausted at the end of the day and more than ready to sit on the porch with Isaac. They shared their days and experiences, or sometimes simply sat in companionable silence. Isaac, with his blonde hair and blue eyes, had been a wonderful companion. His broad frame made him a capable workman, and there was no better feeling than his strong arms around her.

But Isaac had been killed in a horse accident several years ago. Abigail, heartbroken, had been happy to jump at the opportunity of opening the bed and breakfast when her father had offered her the use of the old farmhouse. She might not have a husband to take care of any longer, and she might never have any children that would need her, but she would have her guests. Abigail truly enjoyed taking care of people, even if they only stayed for a day or two.

It might have been a lonely venture for her, but Abigail knew that she could always count on the strength of her family around her. The most help she had invariably came from Amos, her sister's son. Young and full of life, Amos was intrigued by the guests that came to the Troyer Farms Bed and Breakfast. At seventeen, he was in his *Rumspringa* and enjoyed learning about the *Englisch* life.

She would have already been done with the decorating if Chaser the cat had not been helping. The scrappy feline, a mop of brown and orange fur that Abigail had found abandoned in a woodpile some years ago, was currently pulling down the greenery that she had so carefully twined around the cards on the mantle. He had already knocked at least two candles out of the windows, although she knew that if she went to the large kitchen at the back of the bed and breakfast she would probably find at least two more on the floor. It was fortunate that she hadn't lit them yet.

"Chaser! You leave that alone, you naughty *katz!*" Abigail rushed across the living room to disentangle the cat from the décor. "With you around, I'll have to nail everything down."

The cat looked up at Abigail with languid yellow eyes, not too intimidated by Abigail's flapping hands. After a moment, he turned and leapt from the shelf, his heavy frame hitting the wooden floor with a thump before he sauntered off to find trouble somewhere else. Chaser did a good job of keeping the mice away from the inn, but he always found ways to make trouble as well.

Shaking her head and returning to her work, Abigail rearranged the garland that Chaser had dislodged and finished her task. She had no guests, for a change, and the heavy winter weather that would likely be coming her way would almost guarantee that she would pass a very quiet and peaceful Christmas season. The Troyer Farm, surrounded by other Amish farms, was far out of the way from any large cities in the Midwest. Only those who had a purpose came through this area, or those who were lost.

Just as Abigail was heading into the kitchen to begin her holiday baking, a heavy knock sounded on the solid oak door. She jumped and whirled back toward the front of the house. She hadn't been expecting any guests, and it was growing late in the evening. She would have already eaten her *nachtesse* if she hadn't been so consumed with the greenery.

"Coming!" she called as she skittered back into the living room and pulled open the door. A man stood on the step, his face grim and tired. He was older than Abigail, probably in his mid-fifties, and he gazed at her with pale blue eyes that sat behind gold wireframe glasses. The stranger was a heavyset man, and he stood with the stiffness of cold despite his wool coat and scarf. He carried a small and battered suitcase in his hand. Snow was just beginning to fall gently from the sky, and the tiny flakes clung to the fabric. His smooth but wrinkled face and the style of his clothing told her instantly that he was *Englisch.*

Abigail opened the door wide, gesturing for him to come in. She didn't know who this man was, but it was obvious that he couldn't stay out in the December cold any longer. "Please, come in. What may I do for you?"

The newcomer trudged rigidly in the door, tracking bits of snow in with him. His shoulders relaxed visibly as the warmth of the fire hit him. "Thank you. I thought if I had to go any farther, I might freeze to death."

Abigail took the man's case gently from his hand and set it by the coat rack. She peeked out the door as she swung it closed, but she saw no sign of transportation. "Have you been walking? Where's your automobile?"

The man shook his head, his jowls wagging. "I'm afraid it broke down a couple miles down the road. I knew that I was too far from a town to turn back the way I came, and I hoped desperately that I would find someone along this road to help me. The sign out by the road for your bed and breakfast here was like a sign from God."

Not willing to waste any more time, Abigail quickly ushered the man across the room toward the hearth. She didn't worry about the wet tracks he was leaving on the floor; she could clean those later. "Let me have your coat, sir. You'll warm up faster."

With movements that seemed to pain him, her guest unbuttoned his coat and laid it in Abigail's waiting arms, followed by his scarf and hat. Underneath, he wore a blue button-down shirt and khakis.

"Your gloves, too. We can set them by the fire to dry." She couldn't quite explain the panic in her chest at the older man's plight. She didn't know him from anyone else, and yet Abigail wanted very much to make him comfortable.

He sat in the chair she offered him and bent down toward his boots, but his cold fingers fiddled numbly with the laces.

"Let me." Abigail quickly untied the laces and pulled the boots off for him, setting them next to the fire as promised. Chaser appeared from under the man's chair to watch the process, batting playfully at his laces until Abigail shooed him away. She stood and turned to the kitchen. "I'll be right back."

Abigail always had a kettle ready and waiting. There was never any telling during the wintertime when she or one of her guests might like a cup of tea or cocoa. She quickly prepared a mug of tea with honey and rushed it back into the living room for the stranger.

Chaser had settled himself happily in the stranger's lap, and gazed up at Abigail with a pleased look in his eyes as she handed the man his tea. The stranger wrapped his fingers around the proffered drink and sank deeper into the cushions of the chair. "I can't thank you enough."

bigail seated herself in the chair opposite the man. "I'm sorry for the cat. Chaser doesn't usually bother with my guests very much." She pursed her lips in thought; that wasn't exactly true. "Well, he likes to try to get in their rooms and go through their things. But I don't think I've ever seen him actually sit on someone's lap like that. He must like you."

The cat responded with a slow blink of his golden eyes, squeezing them shut happily as he cuddled against the newest guest.

The stranger smiled and removed one hand from his tea mug to stroke the cat, who began purring loudly. "I don't mind at all. I'll take any warmth I can get at this point." He smiled wanly at the creature before looking back up at Abigail with a startled expression in his eyes. "I'm sorry; I never introduced myself. My name is Daniel Bradford."

"It's very nice to meet you, Mr. Bradford," Abigail replied with a nod. "I'm Abigail Lapp. And I'm very happy that you happened to find my inn. We haven't had much snow yet, but the temperatures have been dropping steadily. As a matter of fact, I'm sure you could have stopped in at any of the other farmhouses along the way. Anyone would have been glad to help you."

Mr. Bradford nodded. "I'm sure you're correct, but I... Well, I felt embarrassed, I suppose. I didn't really like the idea of needing to find help."

Abigail waved off his concerns. "There's no need to be ashamed. These things happen. Perhaps it was God's will. At least you're here now instead of walking through the cold."

"Yes," the man agreed uncertainly, "although I suppose I'll still have to get the car taken care of. Do you have a phone?"

The innkeeper shook her head. "No, I'm sorry. We have a community phone just down the road at the corner, though. Perhaps tomorrow I can show you the way, and you can have someone fetch the car. I imagine the garages are closed by now, anyway."

Mr. Bradford looked slightly startled when Abigail said she had no phone, but then he began to study the room he was in. He took in the oil lamps, the stone fireplace, the hardwood floors that had been worn to a shine over the years. His aquamarine eyes then turned to Abigail's plain gray dress, her simple white apron, and her modest cap. "You're very lucky, do you know that?"

Abigail tilted her head, surprised by this statement. Most of the *Englisch* people that she had met, while they understood and perhaps even enjoyed her way of life for a short time, were eager to return to their television sets, automobiles, and central climate control. "I beg your pardon?"

"Forgive me." Mr. Bradford set his tea on the side table and ran his hands over his face. Abigail noticed how careworn his features seemed. "I suppose that wouldn't make sense from a man like me. But by living the way you do, you miss out on so much chaos that the rest of us are forced into. People who aren't Amish—English, I understand you call us —are obligated to keep up with technology and progress whether we want to or not. Otherwise, we fall behind the times and are considered outdated and useless, much like technology itself."

Abigail was confused. Perhaps the man had been out in the cold longer than she realized. "Do you not enjoy your lifestyle? I may sound ignorant, but I understood that most *Englisch* are happy to live the way they do. Certainly, they enjoy taking a peek at a different way of life, but most of them at least miss their televisions and their phones by the time they leave."

Mr. Bradford took his glasses off and frowned as he cleaned them on his shirttail. "I enjoyed it once, when I was a younger man. I was eager to see what science and medicine could bring to the world. Much of it was good, but you can't have the good without the bad. Now that I'm older, I often think that it would have been better to live a simpler life."

"Surely you could still change that, if you wanted to," Abigail offered. Mr. Bradford was not exactly young, but he had plenty of life in him yet. "There is a farm just a few miles down the road that has been taken over by an *Englisch* man. He lives much as we do."

"I'm afraid that it wouldn't be so simple for me." Mr. Bradford reached a wide hand into his pants pocket and retrieved a tiny silver case. The round container shone in the firelight, glancing off his initials on the lid. "You see, the world has already caught up with me. I must take medicine for my heart. It's modern medicine and technology that keep me alive, and that also prevents me from living." He sighed as he put the pill case back in his pocket. "Even if it was possible, I don't know that I would be able to stop other folks from changing my life for me."

Abigail watched with a sad interest as the older man studied the tiny box in his hand. She wished that she could help him. At the very least she could provide him with a cozy room for the night, and she told him so. "You can have your pick of any of the upstairs rooms," she explained. "I don't have any guests at the moment. Just be sure to take a lamp with you so you can see your way around. I'll have breakfast ready by seven-thirty, but I'll be up long before that. If you're an early riser, feel free to come down and sit by the fire. Then I'll be happy to help you get back on the road to— I'm sorry; where were you headed?"

Mr. Bradford gazed into the fire, the flames dancing in the reflection on his glasses. "I want to find a nice place to retire. Somewhere out of the way, where I can get away from the hassles of big city living and yet still have access to good doctors."

"Forgive me for saying so, Mr. Bradford, but it sounds to me like you're already there." Abigail had never traveled too far from their settlement in central Illinois, but she couldn't imagine anyplace better for a person seeking solace. "Our hospital may be small and we have simple country doctors, but I find it rather peaceful."

Again came that sad smile from her new guest. "I'll consider it, Ms. Lapp."

"Please, call me Abigail."

"Thank you, Abigail. For now, I think I'll go to bed." Mr. Bradford had to displace Chaser before he could get up. The cat was a limp bundle of fur as the older man lifted him from his lap and placed him on the hearth. Chaser accepted the change of setting and curled up on the flagstone, falling asleep again within moments.

Mr. Bradford himself looked ready to do the same thing. He fetched his suitcase and headed for the stairs. He laid a hand on the carved wooden bannister before turning back to his hostess. "Good night, Abigail. And thank you again."

"You're very welcome, Mr. Bradford." Abigail watched as he clumped up the stairs one at a time, his burden far heavier than the suitcase in his hand. She returned to her seat by the fire, too intrigued by the strange case of Mr. Bradford to go back to her original plan of baking. The pies and cakes she had planned could wait until tomorrow.

She wanted to take care of Mr. Bradford just like she would for any other guest, but it was clear that this particular guest was in need of more. She only wished she knew how to provide it. Not for the first time, she wished that Isaac was still around. He would have had advice beyond his years for the *Englisch* man as well as for Abigail. But there was nothing to be done about that.

Abigail banked the fire, blew out the remaining lamps, and went to bed. Chaser unfurled himself and followed her to her bedroom on the back side of the house, where he would pass the night at the foot of her bed.

CHAPTER THREE

Abigail rose early as always and looked out the window. She had never needed a clock to let her know when it was time to arise; her body simply knew when morning came. The snow that had begun the evening before now clung as a thin cloak to the ground outside. It was a promise of more to come, but it frosted the trees and the grass beautifully. It would not yet make the farm work difficult, and she was grateful for it.

It had grown chilly in her room overnight and she dressed quickly, eager to pull her warm wool stockings over her feet. Chaser was not eager to get out of bed, but he plopped to the floor and followed her to the kitchen. The cat curled his furry body up next to the wood stove as soon as Abigail had it lit.

Humming to herself as she worked, Abigail began making breakfast for herself and Mr. Bradford. The old man had seemed so grateful for a simple cup of tea, and he was sure to enjoy her breakfast casserole. It was obvious from his paunch that he enjoyed good food, and the innkeeper was always pleased to cook for someone besides herself. Chaser understood this and twirled around Abigail's ankles as she browned sausage on the stove. She shouldn't give him any, lest she discourage him from catching mice, but he usually managed to get a few tidbits out of her.

Abigail added chopped onions to the sausage and let them cook while she prepared a simple dough and spread it in the bottom of the pan. The sausage and onion mixture went on top of the dough along with cheese, diced red peppers, and cubed potatoes. Next, she cracked several brown eggs that had come from the Troyer Farms. The milk she mixed them with had also come from the farm. This went over the top of the casserole, was topped with another layer of cheese, and then went into the oven.

As the scent of the dish began to take over the kitchen, Abigail found the rest of the applesauce bread she had made the day before. It would make a nice side to the casserole, and she eagerly waited for her guest to come down the stairs.

But first, Amos came in the back door with a load of firewood. *"Gute mariye,"* he greeted her as he stacked the wood carefully next to the stove. He had to avoid the cat as he worked, who did not bother getting out of the way. "What work do you have for me this morning?"

Abigail shook her head as she put a pot of coffee on the stove. "There isn't much. I have only one guest at the moment."

Amos finished stacking the wood and straightened up. He was a tall young man with a slim body that belied his strength. He had his mother's sharp hazel eyes under heavy brows, and he never missed a thing. His cheeks were ruddy on their own and made pinker by the cool morning air.

"One?" he asked. "I didn't realize that. I thought you were empty."

"It wasn't until late last evening. A man came in when it was nearly dark. His vehicle had broken down, and he had walked several miles in the cold. He looked ready to freeze to death!" Abigail laid plates and forks out on the table; she always ate with her guests when she could, and Amos often would join them as well. Even if the boy had already eaten breakfast, he would likely accept another round. "Actually, that's what I might need you to do for me. When Mr. Bradford comes downstairs, you can help him make arrangements for his vehicle. You know more about these things than I do."

Her nephew enjoyed visiting the *Englisch* at the garage in town and talking to them about their *kaere.* Amos nodded eagerly, nearly knocking the straw hat off his head. "I'd be happy to. Do you know where it is?"

"I didn't ask him specifically," Abigail replied. "He only said that it was a couple miles down the road. I'm sure Mr. Bradford can tell you. Or, if he's feeling up to it, perhaps you can take him in a buggy to find it."

Amos peeked in the oven at the breakfast casserole until Abigail swatted him away. "Is he sick?" he asked.

Abigail checked the casserole herself. It would be ready in just a few minutes. "Not exactly. But he told me that he has heart trouble, and I'm sure he didn't feel well after his journey on foot."

The young man looked through the kitchen doorway toward the stairs, impatient for the guest to come down and join them. "Is he a late sleeper?"

The innkeeper let out a laugh. "I can't say that I know, can I? It's his first night here. But I did tell him he could come down for breakfast. I'll just run up and check on him."

Upstairs, Abigail realized that she didn't know which room Mr. Bradford had chosen. All of the doors remained closed, and the old man had likely paid attention to what Abigail had said about the cat coming in to satisfy his curiosity. But her guest had been tired, and she didn't imagine that he had roved through the rooms until he found the one that he liked the best.

She knocked on the first door on the right. "Mr. Bradford? Breakfast is ready." There was no reply from the other side of the door. Tentatively, she turned the knob and poked her head inside. She realized that she should have sent Amos on this errand in case the *Englisch* man was in a state of undress. But the room was empty.

Next, Abigail tried the first room on the left. Again, there was no reply to her knock and announcement of breakfast. The scent of the casserole had drifted up the stairs now, and it was likely that her guest already knew it was time to eat if he was awake. She opened the door to this room and gasped.

Mr. Bradford had indeed chosen the first room on the left. He had set the oil lamp on the table next to the bed, and his shoes stood neatly next to one another just under the mattress. But he lay on top of the quilts, fully clothed. His eyes were closed under his glasses and his skin was a horrifically pale shade around his blue lips.

"Mr. Bradford? Sir?" No longer worried about propriety, the innkeeper rushed to the man's side. She laid her hand on his, but it was cold to the touch. Abigail quickly touched her fingers to Mr. Bradford's neck, but she couldn't find a pulse.

Retreating from the room, she rushed back down the stairs and into the kitchen.

Amos was bent over, carefully removing the casserole from the oven. He nearly dropped it when he saw Abigail's face. "What's the matter? What's wrong?"

Wringing her hands in her apron, Abigail fought back tears. She didn't know the man upstairs very well, but she would have liked to. "I think Mr. Bradford is dead," she squeaked.

Her nephew needed no more information before he went rushing up the stairs himself. Abigail waited nervously below as she listened to his footsteps, and he returned only a minute later with a somber look on his young face.

"I think you're right," he affirmed. "What should we do?"

In the five years Abigail had been running the Troyer Farms Bed and Breakfast, she had never had such a thing happen. A few guests had come down with colds or stomach flu, and one child had fallen down the steps and broken her wrist. But a dead man in her guest room was completely new. "He's *Englisch*. I would guess that means we need to call the sheriff."

"I'll do it," Amos volunteered. He strode toward the back door but paused. "Will you be all right if I leave you here? I can fetch my *mudder* to come and stay with you first."

Abigail brushed off his worries. It was a shock to find her guest in such a state, but she had no reason to be afraid or unnerved. "It's okay. I appreciate you making the phone call." She knew that Amos normally enjoyed using the telephone, but it wouldn't be much fun on this particular occasion.

The young man nodded lugubriously and left.

It didn't take long for an ambulance to arrive with a squad car in tow. Abigail showed the paramedics the room her guest was in, and then stood back out of the way while they examined him.

The sheriff's deputy tipped his hat at her kindly. Abigail had never had many run-ins with the police; she had very little reason to in her quiet community. Still, she was relieved to see the kind and sympathetic look in his jade green eyes as he introduced himself. He was the sort of man who looked like he had spent his time in the country, with broad shoulders and weathered cheeks.

"I'm Deputy Tynes. Can you tell me what happened here?"

Abigail twisted her hands in her apron as she recounted the tale of the stranger at her door the previous evening. She made sure to tell him how cold he had been and how Mr. Bradford carried a case of heart medicine in his pocket.

The deputy nodded as she spoke, making notes on a small pad. He glanced down at her hands, which had nearly twisted her apron into a knot. "Don't worry, Ms. Lapp. We'll get everything taken care of. Now, I hate to ask this, but do you have any reason to believe that there might have been foul play? Did Mr. Bradford say anything about having any enemies?"

Abigail reeled in shock. She hadn't even imagined such a thing and didn't like the idea of the possibility under her roof. "Not at all. He mentioned wanting to find a nice quiet place to retire, but I've heard that from other guests many times. He'd lived a complicated life, he said, and wanted something simpler." She pursed her lips, trying to recall any further details from their conversation that she might have missed.

The lawman continued to scribble on his notepad. "And was there anyone else here last night? Did you hear any suspicious noises?"

Abigail shook her head. "It was just the two of us, and it was very quiet. He was up in his room, and I was in my room at the back of the house." She gestured over her shoulder in the direction of her chamber.

Just then, one of the paramedics emerged from Mr. Bradford's bedroom and came downstairs into the living room. He approached the deputy. "It looks like it was probably a heart attack," he explained, confirming Abigail's guess. "He had a prescription for heart meds, and at the moment I don't have any reason to believe it was anything other than a natural death."

The deputy made note of it, and the paramedic ascended the stairs once more to remove the body from the room. Abigail watched with a heavy heart as the uniformed men brought Mr. Bradford down on a gurney—no small task on those stairs—and covered with a sheet. She wished she could have at least had a chance to tell him goodbye.

One of the paramedics tripped on the last step, dropping his corner of the gurney. Abigail brought her fist to her mouth, terrified that Mr. Bradford's body would roll to the floor. Deputy Tynes jumped forward, ready to grab the stretcher. But the other technicians made up for the mistake and kept the gurney straight. They carried him the rest of the way out of the bed and breakfast without incident.

Deputy Tynes turned to Abigail before he left. "If there's anything else you need, don't hesitate to let me know." He produced a business card from his pocket and handed it to her.

Abigail took it, but hoped that she wouldn't need it. "Thank you for coming so quickly." She stopped him as he turned back toward the door. "Oh! I just remembered. I don't think anything has been done about his car yet. My nephew was going to help Mr. Bradford get it to a garage, but needless to say we got a little distracted."

The officer gave her a reassuring smile. "We'll find it and get it taken care of."

When everyone was out of the house and the emergency vehicles had cleared the driveway, Abigail stood in stunned silence and listened to the hush that had taken over the inn. Normally she appreciated such peace, but today it was a quiet that resulted from the death of a kind man. A shiver made its way down her spine despite the crackling of the fire.

Returning to the kitchen to finally eat her breakfast, Abigail noticed a crumpled piece of paper at the bottom of the stairs. It must have fallen out of Mr. Bradford's pocket when the paramedic almost dropped him. She picked it up, but she didn't have the heart to look at it. She stuffed it in her apron and did her best to go about her day.

CHAPTER FOUR

Amos returned as Abigail sat down at the table with a slice of her breakfast casserole. "What did they say?" He helped himself to a slice of the dish and seated himself across from her. "I would have been back sooner, but I kept running into others that were curious as to what was happening. My mother was one of them, and she had a few chores for me as well."

Abigail nodded her understanding. There was nothing Amos could have done for her anyway, and he had probably provided the most help by staving off any inquisitive onlookers. "They said it was a heart attack, which wasn't a surprise. But it is a shame."

"I would have liked to have seen them in action. We don't have flashing lights and sirens very often here."

The breakfast casserole didn't taste as good as Abigail had expected; her tongue seemed unwilling to acknowledge it. She pushed it away slightly and rested her hands on the table. "You should be grateful for that. They have their job to do and I'm glad they did it, but I can't say that I enjoyed it."

"I'm sorry. I didn't mean it like that. I know you're upset." He gulped down the rest of his meal and stood. "Are you expecting any other boarders today?"

Abigail shrugged. "None that I know of. I think we'll have a few coming in later in the month, but nothing other than that."

"Good. Then that should free me up to assist Vaader with the cattle today. We're moving them to a different pasture for the winter, and Abram Miller is bringing in another load of hay to stack in the barn." He paused for a moment, his eyes pale in the winter light as he looked thoughtfully out the back window. "You could always come to the main house, if you don't want to be here alone. I'm sure *mudder* would keep you busy."

Abigail couldn't help but snicker. Her sister was known for being a talkative, busy person. She would no doubt sit Abigail down at the table and talk incessantly while darning socks for the entire community. It was more than she felt like enduring at the moment, but it was sweet of Amos to be so concerned for her. "Thank you, but I have a few things I want to get done around here while it isn't busy. I never did get around to my baking."

At this, Amos grinned. "Will that include one or two of your famous apple pies?"

Abigail smiled back. "Of course. And I'll be sure to save some for you."

When Amos was gone, Abigail was faced with a task that she did not look forward to. The emergency medical technicians had taken care of Mr. Bradford's body, but his room still needed to be looked after. As much as she didn't want to go in there, she couldn't leave it the way it was. If she had asked him, Amos would have taken on the task without question. But Abigail couldn't ask him to do such a thing. There were some chores she had to do herself.

For the second time that day, Abigail plodded up the stairs. The paramedics had left the door ajar, and she pushed it open slowly. The cool December light came through the window and illuminated the interior of the small room. Though Mr. Bradford had never gotten under the covers, the quilts were rumpled. His boots remained on the floor, but the emergency staff had bumped them. Instead of being neatly aligned under the edge of the bed, they were on their sides and sitting askew.

Abigail came fully into the room and set to work. She removed the bedding and brought it downstairs to be laundered. Next, she filled a bucket with hot soapy water and took it and the mop upstairs. The floor wasn't truly dirty, but the room deserved a thorough cleaning.

She set the mop and bucket down while she dusted the furniture with a rag. On the other side of the bed, away from the door, she discovered Mr. Bradford's suitcase. Abigail had completely forgotten about it. The case sat flat on the floor with the latches undone. The innkeeper opened it tentatively, finding that almost nothing was inside. She then began to go methodically through the drawers of the dresser, retrieving two shirts, a pair of pants, several mismatched socks, and a Bible. She smiled at the knowledge that Mr. Bradford had been a Godly man. He had very little with him, and the clothing didn't look as though it matched.

As she picked up his Bible to lay it in the suitcase, a rectangle of paper fluttered out of it and to the floor. Picking it up and turning it over, she discovered that it was a photograph. Abigail studied the picture for a moment. It looked old; a fact that Abigail could easily verify by the fact that one of the men in the picture was a much younger version of Daniel Bradford. There were several other men with him, standing together on a grassy lawn with a small house in the background. The subjects squinted into the sun as they put their arms on each other's shoulders. Abigail hoped that a family member would show up for his belongings, and that she would be able to return such a precious thing. As an Amish woman, Abigail had never had her picture taken. She did, however, understand just how important a photo like this might be to Mr. Bradford's family.

With everything packed back into the suitcase, Abigail took it and his boots to the closet in the upstairs hallway. She placed them inside for safekeeping, then fetched his coat and scarf from the coatrack downstairs by the front door and put them with his other belongings until she could find out what to do with them.

Abigail's cleaning of Mr. Bradford's room soon spread to the rest of the house. As she dumped the steaming mop water off the side of the porch, she decided that the rest of the place could use a good scrubbing as well. She even got down on her hands and knees to make sure the corners were clean. It was therapeutic, cleaning out her mind as she cleaned her home and business. By the time she was finished, her knees were sore and her hands were chapped, but she felt much better.

Amos arrived just before suppertime. He stood next to the

wood stove in the kitchen to warm him himself as he shared the news he had discovered. "I was busy with the cattle and the hay today, so I didn't think about Mr. Bradford's car until just a couple of hours ago. I asked around, and I found out that it had already been taken to the garage."

Though the car had truly never been her problem, Abigail was relieved to hear this. "Good. The sheriff's department must have taken care of it. I told Deputy Tynes that it was on the side of the road."

Amos nodded. "Well, you know how I am. I was curious as to what was wrong with it, so I went to talk to the mechanics. They showed it to me, and the whole front end of it was crumpled."

Abigail had been stirring a pot of stew, but she laid down her wooden spoon and gave Amos her full attention. "Really? He never said that he wrecked it."

The young man raised his thick eyebrows. "That's the thing. The mechanics said that when their tow truck found the car, it had been run into an embankment. They checked it over at the request of the sheriff, and the brake lines were cut."

"What does that mean?" Abigail asked with a furrowed brow. She didn't share her nephew's fascinations for automobiles.

Amos ran his hand over his forehead, concerned over the information he had learned. "It means that someone had sabotaged his automobile so that he would have a wreck. The men down at the car shop were going crazy over it. They said that it's the sort of thing they see in movies, but none of them had ever seen it in real life."

Abigail plunked down in a kitchen chair. "Who would want to kill Mr. Bradford? He was such a sweet man." She felt dizzy at the thought. It was bad enough to have one of her lodgers pass away, but it was a whole other thing to think they might have been murdered.

"Your guess is as good as anyone else's at this point," Amos admitted. "Of course they have reported this to the sheriff's department. I imagine that Deputy Tynes will be back to ask you more questions."

This concerned Abigail even more. Her heart pounded in her chest. "You aren't saying that they're going to accuse me, are you? I did nothing but try to help the man."

The young man laid a hand on her shoulder. "I'm sure they won't, but you were the only other person here with Mr. Bradford and the last person to see him alive. You're at least the first place for them to start. But don't worry; I'm happy to be here with you."

A knock sounding on the door cut their discussion short. Abigail jumped. "That's probably him."

"I'll let him in," Amos volunteered.

But instead of a uniformed officer, an elderly couple stood on the porch. They were *Englisch*, and they smiled happily at Amos and Abigail, who was standing behind him.

"We're sorry to disturb you," said the man. He was bundled up in a coat with numerous buttons and zippers. A knit cap slouched down over his eyes, which were the same gray as his shaggy hair. "We are traveling through on our way to visit our family for the holidays, and we were wondering if you have any rooms available. We'd like to take shelter before the weather gets too bad."

Amos, as surprised as Abigail had been when the knock

came, didn't hesitate to step back and let them in the door. "Please, come in."

Abigail rushed to their sides and took their coats. "I do have rooms available. Almost all of them, in fact! And you're just in time for supper, if you haven't eaten yet."

"Oh, that would be wonderful," the woman replied. Her coat was bright pink and very puffy, making her look like a piece of candy. A matching pair of earmuffs had been settled down over her pouf of gray hair. "We haven't eaten for hours, and the road has been a long one since our last stop."

"Come on in, then. I think the stew is about ready. My name is Abigail Lapp, and this is my nephew Amos."

The man nodded in greeting. "I'm James Mitchell, and this is my wife Diane. We're from Indiana." He gratefully seated himself at the table, where Abigail was busy setting out plates, napkins, and forks. "We were very glad to see your sign. If we hadn't happened to come right by here, there's no telling how much longer we would have had to go."

"I wouldn't want to be out after dark, either," Diane chimed in. "We've done that when we've had to, but it's particularly dangerous in the winter."

"I'm very glad you came upon us," Abigail agreed. "I can smell snow on the air; I'm sure it will be coming soon. But we have a nice warm fire and plenty of food. Amos, would you please bring in their luggage."

CHAPTER FIVE

Abigail easily slipped back into the routine of taking care of her guests. Her heart warmed as she and Amos worked together to make them comfortable. Her nephew jumped at her word, fetching their numerous pieces of matching luggage from the trunk of their sedan.

"Give them the room on the right," Abigail murmured as he passed her to head to the second floor. She didn't want there to be any chance of the Mitchells staying in the same room Daniel Bradford had been in, but she could also justify a prettier view of the farm from the windows on the right side of the hallway.

"Is there anything I can do to help?" Diane Mitchell asked as Abigail returned to the kitchen to begin dishing out the stew.

"Thank you, but I think it's just about ready to go. I have only to take the biscuits out of the oven, and we'll be ready to eat." She pulled open the oven door, relishing in the scent of the hot bread. The tops were crispy and golden, promising soft centers. The innkeeper enjoyed this type of meal herself, and she was excited to share it with her guests.

Chaser, too, was happy at the new company. He must have missed having Mr. Bradford's lap to cuddle on, and he was busy strutting back and forth underneath the dining table. He ran his cheek against Mrs. Mitchell's ankles before trotting over to her husband to do the same. The couple didn't seem to mind, and Abigail wouldn't be surprised if several scraps of beef managed to make their way out of the stew pot and into the cat's belly.

Just as she turned to the table with the pot of stew, another pounding came at the door. Abigail nearly dropped their supper in surprise. She managed to recover it with only burning her pinkie finger.

James Mitchell, reading the shock on his hostess's face, asked, "Were you expecting anyone else?"

Abigail appreciated his concern. The man already knew that Abigail hadn't planned for even the two of them. It was his way of asking if everything was okay. But she couldn't quite have explained to him the unsettled feeling that once again rattled its way inside her at the sound of yet someone else at the door.

"I'll get it," Amos volunteered.

Abigail waved him back into his seat. She couldn't take any more anticipation. "No, no. I can do it."

He knew better than to argue with her, and he remained at the table.

Her heart pounded in her chest as she crossed to the front of the bed and breakfast. The sound of her boots on the hard wooden floors sounded like echoes of the knock that had come only a moment before. Normally, she was more than happy to find new tenants at her door. They were a source of income, good conversation, and fulfilling work that she could be proud of. How could this be any different?

Besides, there was always the chance that the person on the other side of that door wasn't a guest at all. Any of her family members from the farm would come in the back door, just like Amos did, but it could have been one of the other neighbors in their community. Perhaps it was Susan King delivering a Christmas pie from her own stash of baked goods, or Josiah Graber coming by to let her know that he had a new batch of wool ready. Though Abigail often visited his shop when she was in need of yarn, he had developed a habit of coming by unexpectedly.

The cat, not intimidated by Abigail's worrisome thoughts, followed along at a jaunty pace. He was eager to find out if the next guest was as interesting as the Mitchells.

But the face that greeted her when she opened the door was not one that she was familiar with. It was not the pale, round face of Susan King nor the shy smiling countenance of Josiah Graber. This man was Amish, but it was not a man in their community. She didn't recognize his long, sharp-featured face under a scraggly beard. He was slim and wiry, his wool coat hanging off his frame. He carried only a small valise. The snow had begun to come down again, the swirling flakes flying angrily down at the stranger and flinging themselves at his cheek. His heavy eyebrows seemed to bear down onto his hard blue eyes. The way he leaned against the doorframe, looming over Abigail, made her want to shrink back in the house and slam the door.

"I'm looking for a room," he demanded. "Do you have any open?"

Abigail studied his face, her body frozen but not by the chill wind that swept in the door and scattered white flakes on the floor. She didn't know him; that much was true. He was dressed like an Amish man, complete with suspenders and straw hat, but he was not someone from this community. This in itself was nothing for her to be suspicious of, and she shook her body to rid herself of needless suspicious feelings. "Um, yes. Yes, I do have rooms available. Won't you come in?"

The newcomer clomped inside, tracking in snow instead of wiping it off his boots on the mat provided for such things. He glared around the living room as though he was looking for something. "Do you have any other guests?"

The innkeeper was distracted from answering his question by the reaction of her cat. Chaser had stopped in his tracks just a few feet behind her, standing completely still. As the new guest entered the room, the cat took several steps in reverse, arched his back, and hissed loudly.

"Bad *katz*!" Abigail admonished, turning to the creature with a pointed finger. "You don't treat our guests that way!"

But Chaser wasn't concerned with manners or the feelings of the latest arrival. His tail was puffed up like a bottlebrush, and the row of hair down his spine was reacting the same way. He was already a fluffy cat as it was, but now he looked like a ball of freshly carded wool. Unable to obey his mistress, Chaser turned tail and ricocheted out of the room.

"I'm sorry," Abigail apologized as she turned back to the man, who was watching the entire exchange with indifference. "Usually he's quite happy to see new people. To answer your question: yes. A couple arrived just a little bit ago. The

Mitchells are already seated at the table, and you're welcome to join us for supper."

The stranger shifted from foot to foot uncomfortably. He made no motions to remove his coat or hat, and he hadn't come any farther in the door than he had to for Abigail to shut it behind him. "I thought this was a bed and breakfast, not a full-service inn."

Abigail ignored the slight. Her guest was correct, even if he was rude. "Normally, yes. There are many good restaurants in town that my tenants often patronize. But with the weather being so nasty, and the fact that everyone is here and supper is already made, I thought it might be a nice idea."

The stranger's hesitation was palpable. It filled the room and choked the air right out of Abigail's lungs. "I ... suppose I could do that." Despite agreeing to the meal, he remained frozen in the entryway.

"Let me take your coat," Abigail suggested.

"No!" He cringed away from her. "I mean, no thank you. I'll get it myself."

When he was down to his shirt and trousers—his hat, coat, and boots all arranged on and underneath the coat rack— Abigail led him into the kitchen. The Mitchells were waiting expectantly at the table, their eyebrows raised and their plates empty. Amos sat on the edge of his chair, looking ready to spring into action any moment. Apparently, the death of Mr. Bradford had made him jumpy as well.

"It looks like we'll have one more guest this evening," Abigail announced to the group. "This is Mr. and Mrs. Mitchell from Indiana, and this is my nephew Amos. Please meet— Oh!" Abigail clapped her hands to her cheeks and turned toward the newcomer. "I'm afraid I never got your name, sir."

"Erm, Jacob. Jacob Sutter." He slowly folded his tall frame into the chair that Abigail pulled up to the table for him before she dashed back to the hutch for another place setting.

"Oh! Any relation to the Sutters from Montgomery?" inquired Mr. Mitchell, leaning forward toward the latest person to the dining table. He had a large belly that rolled over onto his lap. "I've met a few of them when I've gone down that way. We always like to travel through Amish country when we get the chance. There's nothing like the honest, simple way that you folks like to live. It's refreshing."

Mr. Sutter sat with his back straight against the wooden back of the chair and eyed his dining companion warily. "No. No, I can't say that I am."

Abigail placed the extra set of dishes down in front of Jacob and gladly began dishing out the stew. Diana picked up the plate of biscuits and passed them around the table, and Abigail's heart once again began to slow down and began beating to the pace of a peaceful wintertime meal. The ice chips that were beginning to pound against the windows couldn't do a thing to them right now, not compared to the warmth of the kitchen and the savory aroma of the stew.

"You know," Diane remarked, continuing the line of thought her husband had been beginning to take, "I grew up living much like the Amish do. We had no electricity, and we had to pump our water by hand. People don't believe me when I tell them that; they think absolutely everyone has grown up with the luxuries of our modern era. But our farm was very rural, and that was just the way it was."

The innkeeper could understand why it was hard to believe that Mrs. Mitchell had ever lived without modern amenities. Her thick cashmere sweater, tailored pants, and the soft boots she had left by the door didn't exactly fit in with a childhood without running water. She wore diamonds that sparkled from her ears, fingers, and around her neck, and there was plenty of makeup on her refined face. This was a woman who had made up for any years of inconvenience she may have had.

But Abigail didn't begrudge her for giving up a way of life that was traditional and meaningful for the Amish. She knew that it wasn't for everyone. "I'm sure that makes you appreciate what you have all the more."

Diane nodded enthusiastically. "Oh, indeed it does! I can't tell you how many winter mornings I wake up and thank the heavens that I don't have frost on the comforter. Don't get me wrong, Ms. Lapp, I very much respect what you people do. It is, as my husband said, refreshing. But I just don't think I'm cut out for it." She turned back to Mr. Sutter. "What about you? Do you ever just wish you could snuggle down under the covers and not get out of bed in the morning?"

If Jacob had seemed slightly uncomfortable before, that had only increased at Diane's question. He sat so stiffly in his chair that he might have been a statue. "No. I know there is always work to be done."

"You ought to be more sensible about these things, dear," James admonished his wife. "They aren't spoiled rotten like you are."

Abigail hid a smile behind her napkin. She liked this couple. They were a good source of entertainment, and they didn't seem to mind that everyone was watching them.

Diane waved her husband's concerns off, nearly tossing her spoon across the room while doing so. "Oh, hush! What do you know? Just because you've hung around a few Amish folks at an auction house or two doesn't make you an expert."

James rolled his eyes and sighed. "I never said it did, my dear. I just wish you would keep quiet and stop embarrassing yourself."

"You think it's embarrassing for me to talk about my childhood? Are you ashamed that you married a woman who once ran barefoot through the dirt and mud with grass in her hair? Well, James Mitchell, you can just get right over it. I might not have had much, but I enjoyed the freedom I had from all the worries in the world. I know a lot more about how the Amish live than you do."

James turned to Abigail, his hand stretched out toward his wife. "I'm so sorry about all of this. I don't want you think poorly of us."

"It's quite all right," Abigail assured him. "Everyone is different and has different views."

Amos, at the end of the table, had been so fascinated by the conversation that he had yet to touch his food. "What made you change your mind?" he asked. "Why did you leave the farm?" Amos was at the age where he would be deciding soon whether or not he would officially join the church. He was allowed to explore the way the *Englisch* lived so that he could come to the church without any doubts when he was ready. Abigail was fairly certain that the young man would choose to stay. After all, all of his friends and family were here, and there was a certain young lady down the road that he seemed interested in. But he was also incredibly captivated by things like electricity, automobiles, and phones.

Mrs. Miller was flattered by the interview, and she now turned her attention to Amos. "Oh, it wasn't really a choice. It's one of those things that just happen to you when you grow up and see how the rest of the world is living. You don't think anything of being dirt poor until you see that other folks aren't. I just had to pull myself up by my bootstraps and head out into the world. I got myself a job off the farm, and I worked my way up the corporate ladder."

"And you didn't miss it at all?" he asked. "I know you said that you enjoy being comfortable, but didn't you miss working with your hands or knowing that you had put in a solid day's work?"

The woman shrugged. "As I said, I just wasn't made for it. I could have married one of the neighboring farmers and stayed out in the wilderness for the rest of my life, but the big city was calling me. And I still did plenty of work, it was just a different sort. Instead of feeding the chickens and shoveling the barn, I was chugging along behind a desk."

Mr. Mitchell cleared his throat. "I'm sure, *dear,* that you don't mean to give the young man the wrong impression. Farm life might not have been for *you,* but city life isn't for other folks, either."

Once again, Abigail smiled at the conversation. Mr. Mitchell was concerned that his wife would influence Amos's decision on joining the church and remaining with the Amish community. Mrs. Mitchell was too wrapped up in herself to notice. Abigail knew that Amos wouldn't be influenced by anyone he didn't want to be, and he was eager to learn everything he could about other ways of life. It was natural for a boy his age.

Suddenly, Diane seemed to realize just what she was telling the boy. She sat up straighter in her chair, her mouth drawn into a small moue. "But I don't think that's for everyone either, honey. I'm sure Mr. Sutter can tell you more about working hard and living a good life than I can." She picked up her mug of tea and buried her face in it.

The diners turned to Jacob, who shifted uneasily in his chair. "There's much to be learned from farm life," he finally said.

"It's a good thing you arrived when you did," Abigail remarked as she filled Jacob's bowl, hoping to find a topic that would make him more comfortable. He was plainly not a man of many words. "I've been expecting the weather to take a turn for the worse, and I believe we're finally going to get a big snow."

"Yes," Diane agreed with a nod, enthusiastic now that the subject of snow and the danger of traveling in it had been brought up once again. "If you had arrived just a few hours later than you had, why you could have been lost in a whiteout!" She split open her biscuit and buttered it generously. "You know, James and I were stuck in a whiteout once. Remember that, dear? When you got us lost on those country roads on the way to my Aunt Cindy's house? I thought we would never come out of it alive."

"I didn't get us lost," her husband retorted. "I knew exactly where we were going."

Mrs. Mitchell nodded. "Oh, I'm sure you did. That's why you were cursing under your breath the entire time and praying for the spring thaw to come early."

James scraped his spoon against the side of his bowl irritably. "We made it, didn't we? And I certainly never hear any offers from you to drive."

This time it was Amos's turn to corral the conversation. "What brings you through this area, anyway?" he asked Mr. Sutter around a bite of potato. "Are you on your way to visit family for the holidays as well?"

Mr. Sutter picked his spoon up and tentatively dipped it into the brown gravy of the thick soup. "No. Yes. I mean, not exactly." He set the spoon back down again and took a deep breath. "I'm sorry. I'm a little out of sorts after all the traveling that I've been doing. I've come this way to look for a friend of mine. I believe he was coming through here, and I hoped to catch up with him."

A chill descended over Abigail despite the warmth of the room. "What is your friend's name?" Silently, she prayed that he would not answer with Daniel Bradford's name.

"Daniel Bradford. Have you seen him?"

The innkeeper could no longer smell the delicious meal, feel the warmth of the fire, or find that cozy feeling in her heart that she had enjoyed only a few minutes ago. "He was here, Jacob. He came through just last night. I'm so sorry to have to be the one to tell you that he passed away from a heart attack."

The newcomer didn't seem surprised by this information. He nodded solemnly and picked up his spoon once again. "He wasn't a well man. He'd been having heart trouble for years. I thought perhaps he would at least get to enjoy his retirement."

But Mrs. Mitchell was far more upset about Mr. Sutter's

friend. "Oh, that's terrible! Why, you poor thing. You've come all this way only to find out that your friend is no longer with us! That's no way to start the holiday season."

"Diane…" warned Mr. Mitchell.

"Really, James! Aren't you listening? His friend died unexpectedly. Why, can you imagine what I would do if Jenny or Rita were to suddenly drop dead? And right before Christmas? I would be absolutely beside myself. I don't think you could even get me out of bed to go shopping for gifts, no matter how cold it was in the house."

Mr. Mitchell glanced up with hooded lids at Mr. Sutter before muttering to his wife once more. "It's his business, dear, not ours. We don't have anything to do with it. Just leave it be."

"Oh, nonsense! Tell us, Mr. Sutter. What was your friend like? Did the two of you grow up together?"

The slim man didn't seem nearly as disturbed by this exchange as Mr. Mitchell did. He shook his head. "We had known each other our entire lives, but we didn't live on the same farm. He was a neighbor, an *Englisch* neighbor."

"Oh, that's so nice." Mrs. Mitchell tipped her head and smiled prettily at Jacob, trying to coax him into talking more. "You don't find friendships like that very often."

Mr. Sutter looked out the window, the swirling snowflakes keeping his attention for a long minute before he replied. "You could say we were like brothers."

CHAPTER SIX

The remainder of the meal passed in more casual conversation. Everyone avoided the topic of Mr. Bradford, not wanting to upset Jacob. Mr. and Mrs. Mitchell calmed their bickering the more they ate. The snow was beginning to accumulate on the window frames, and when Abigail stood to take the dishes to the sink she saw that the world was completely covered in white. It was not the dusting they'd had the day before, but a full-on snowstorm.

The *Englisch* guests she had spoken to in the past, much like Diane, were intimidated by a blizzard. It meant that travel became difficult or even impossible, and sometimes their phone lines went down as well. It meant being cut off from the rest of the world. While that may be too much for some to handle, Abigail found it relaxing. There was no obligation to do anything but stay indoors and enjoy their time together.

Abigail plunged the dishes into a sink of hot, soapy water to let them soak before dishing out the remainder of the applesauce cake. It would have been nice if Mr. Bradford could have had some of it with them, but at least she would be able to serve it to his friend and her guests. And at the very least, none of it would go to waste.

As she returned to the dining table, Mr. Mitchell was once again trying to engage Jacob in conversation. "Tell me, Mr. Sutter. What do you do for a living? I understand that some of the Amish have shifted away from the farm life and run stores or even work in factories."

Jacob nodded slowly as he mulled over the question. "That's true, I suppose. I have a furniture store."

Mr. Mitchell bobbed his head earnestly. "Wonderful. Amish-made furniture is the best around. I have a beautiful entertainment center that I bought on one of our trips into Amish country. I thought it a bit ironic, since you folks don't watch television. How do you reconcile things like that? I mean, does it bother you to make something like that when it's going to be used in conjunction with things like electricity and television?"

Mr. Sutter didn't have the chance to reply. Abigail had just set the plates of applesauce cake on the table when yet another knock came at the front door. She didn't bother to worry about it this time. Everything had been going smoothly, despite the constant chatter of the Mitchells and the quiet conservatism of Jacob.

Deputy Tynes, a heavy coat with a fur collar covering his uniform, waited for her on the other side of the door. His green eyes were bright and urgent against the backdrop of the snowy evening. "I'm sorry to bother you. Can I come in for a moment?"

"Of course." Abigail showed him in and was about to offer

him a slice of cake, but the look on his face implied that what he had to say was too pressing to wait for dessert.

He led her by the elbow to the fireplace in the living room, which was at the opposite end from the doorway to the kitchen. His voice was low and gravelly. "I see you have some visitors, so I'll try to keep this brief and quiet. I came to tell you that we got the autopsy results back on Daniel Bradford. It turns out that it wasn't a heart attack at all."

Abigail's throat went dry, and it wasn't from being in such close proximity to the fireplace. "What was it then?" She didn't want to know the answer, but it was too late to pretend she could avoid this.

Deputy Tynes took a deep breath and puffed it out through his cheeks. "He was poisoned. Those pills in his pocket weren't heart medicine at all. An official investigation into his homicide has just opened up."

"This can't be happening." Putting one hand to her head, Abigail leaned heavily on the bookshelves that flanked the fireplace on both sides. "I should have seen it coming, though. Amos told me about his vehicle being tampered with."

The officer's frown deepened, and it matched a downward vee in his forehead. "How does he know about that?"

"It's a small town, and he likes to visit with the mechanics. I'm sorry, Deputy, but that's not the sort of thing that can be kept secret for very long. I won't say anything about the pills, but I'm sure you know that everyone else will find out in due time."

"I'm afraid you're right," the deputy replied grimly. "I know it's a lot to absorb for folks around here, and people can't help but gossip a little. I promise you I'll keep you posted as things progress. You were the only one in this area who had spoken with him, or at least the only one we know of."

Abigail perked up. "Actually, another one just arrived. Jacob Sutter just arrived, and he said he was *friend* with Mr. Bradford. The two of them grew up together. Maybe he can give you some more information."

The lawman seemed hesitant. "I don't want to break up your dinner party, but it might be helpful if I could get some information from him. Besides, I'm not sure when I'll be able to get back out here. My car barely got through the snow as it was."

Abigail peeked through the doorway to the kitchen. "Jacob, the deputy that handled Mr. Bradford's case is here. He'd like to speak with you for a moment."

Mr. Sutter's eyes widened visible under his heavy brows, but he stood and came slowly into the living room, where Abigail introduced the two men.

"I'll leave the two of you be. Unless, Deputy, I can get you a hot drink?"

Deputy Tynes was busy fishing his notebook and a stubby pencil out of the pocket of his coat. "Thank you, ma'am, but I'll have to pass for the moment."

Abigail returned to the table for her own slice of cake, but she was desperately curious what the two men in the living room were saying to each other. It wasn't any of her business, but she wanted to get to the bottom of Mr. Bradford's murder just as badly as the police did. He had died under her roof, after all. Perhaps if she knew more details, she could help Deputy Tynes figure it out. It would put her mind at ease, and maybe Jacob's as well.

She shook her head at her silly thoughts. The policeman wouldn't want to have a simple Amish widow working on his latest case. It was probably going to be a big one for him, too, since things like homicides didn't happen around here very often. No, it was best for her to just cooperate with him as best she could and let him do his job.

"Is everything all right?" Mr. Mitchell whispered across the table. "I don't think I've ever seen the police at an Amish home before."

Abigail mustered up a smile for her guest. "Yes, everything is fine. He's just here to talk to Jacob, since he was friends with Mr. Bradford. And that's true; we don't have the police in our community very often. But I know they have stopped to help my neighbors when a wheel broke on their buggy, and of course they had to get involved since Mr. Bradford was *Englisch*. They've been very helpful so far."

"They must have a different outlook here than they do in the cities," Diane mused. "They think everyone is a criminal where I come from. I wouldn't dare speed, because I wouldn't want to go through the torture of getting pulled over."

Abigail widened her eyes at this revelation. She had not had to deal with the police personally until just recently, but she had often seen them in town at the shops or restaurants. They always smiled and said hello, and she had never thought of them as anything but another aspect of their rural community.

"It's not that bad," James corrected her. "And you speed all the time."

Jacob came back to the table just then, and Abigail left the Mitchells to inquisition him while she went back to the living room to see if the deputy needed anything else. He still stood in front of the fireplace, staring into the flames.

"I hope that was helpful," she said as she approached. "I know it isn't my business, but I would very much like to know what happened to Mr. Bradford."

Deputy Tynes shrugged. "He didn't really have any information that was pertinent, but it didn't hurt to ask. Do you still have any of Mr. Bradford's belongings?"

The innkeeper dutifully fetched the suitcase she had been holding in her upstairs closet, along with the boots and coat. As she came back down the stairs, the latch on the case broke. The lid split open, causing all of the dead man's belongings to spill out. They cascaded down the stairs toward the floor.

"Oh, no!" Abigail exclaimed as she stooped to gather the clothing and other items that were now everywhere. "I'm so sorry.

The deputy, upon hearing the crash, dashed across the room to assist her. "Don't be sorry. These things happen."

"I took everything out of his room after you left the last time, and I kept it just in case you needed it," Abigail explained as she replaced Mr. Bradford's Bible in the suitcase. "Of course, at that time, I thought the only reason you would need it would be to return it to his family members. I suppose now you'll be looking for clues?"

He smiled at her curiosity. "Yes, I guess so. I don't know how much I'll find out from some mismatched clothing, but you never know."

The photo that had caught Abigail's attention before was now on the bottom step. She picked it up gently by the corner and studied it once again. One of the men in the picture looked familiar, but she couldn't quite put her finger on it. There was no time to ponder it, though, because the deputy was waiting for her to place it in the case. "I can get you a bit of string to tie that together with," she offered.

"Thank you. It wouldn't help much if I dropped it all in the snow."

Once she had the suitcase securely tied, she walked Deputy Tynes back to the door. He paused before opening it and looked back at her. "Do me a favor, Ms. Lapp. Be careful."

"Do you think there's a need for me to?" Abigail hadn't thought about this. She had been concerned for what might have happened to Daniel Bradford, but she had never truly imagined that the danger extended to her as well.

He picked an imaginary piece of lint from his coat. "I don't know. I wish I could tell you something specific, but I really just don't know anything. In the meantime, I just want you to be safe."

"Thank you, Deputy. I will."

When she retreated once again to the kitchen, Jacob excused himself and went upstairs to bed.

CHAPTER SEVEN

Abigail lay awake in bed that night, her eyes wide against sleep. Once dinner and dessert had been done, she had watched through the kitchen window as Amos and the lantern he carried travelled across the yard to his mother's house, so she knew he was safely at home. The Mitchells had stayed up only long enough for a mug of hot apple cider by the fireplace before they went to bed as well, citing their extensive day of traveling for making them so tired. Abigail knew they probably just didn't want to feel like a burden on her.

She had only seen Jacob for a moment as he left the kitchen and retired for the evening, leaving half of his applesauce cake still on his plate. Abigail didn't blame him; in the span of less than an hour he had discovered not only that his good friend had passed away but that he had probably been murdered as well. That was enough to make anyone skip dessert and go to bed.

The innkeeper herself had endured a busy and exhaustive day. It should have been easy for her to drift off into a dreamless sleep, but her mind wouldn't stop ticking through every random event of the day. Snippets of conversations, looks on her guests faces, and the contents of Mr. Bradford's suitcase rolled through her mind.

She hummed hymns that she had known since she was a child, counted out on her fingers how many different kinds of cakes and pies she wanted to make for the holidays, and mused about how much the snow on the rooftop must weigh. But none of that could truly distract her from the mysterious case of Mr. Daniel Bradford.

Why would someone want to kill such a nice man? Who would have switched out his heart medicine for poison, and when would they have been able to do such a thing? Was it the same person who had cut his brake lines?

With a sudden clarity that she hadn't had all day, Abigail wondered why someone would go to the trouble to both poison him and sabotage his automobile. That seemed like a bit much. Wouldn't just one or the other have been enough? But no, she realized instantly that that line of thinking wasn't correct. If the brake lines were enough, then Mr. Bradford wouldn't ever have made it to the Troyer Farms Bed and Breakfast.

That brought her back to the deputy's warning just before he had left that evening. She wished she had thought to ask him more questions. Did he think there was a specific motive behind Daniel's murder? Or was it something more random? Surely, if the murderer had gone to the trouble of obtaining poisoned pills that looked just like the man's heart medicine, then this was all part of a grander scheme. But then why would Deputy Tynes be concerned for Abigail's safety?

She had a feeling there was something he wasn't telling her, but then again, that was the way it probably ought to be. If she knew everything the police did, then she might be putting herself in harm's way. She would be glad to do so if it solved the mystery around her guest's death, but it was apparent that the officer didn't want that to happen.

Sometime in the wee hours, she had finally drifted off to sleep. Her dreams were full of strange faces, eerie noises, and applesauce cake. At one point, she dreamed that she had so many guests at her door that she didn't have room for them all and had to turn them away.

Her natural internal alarm clock did not go off in the morning. The heavy snow on the ground and the clouds that it had fallen from made for a dark atmosphere, barely letting the early morning sunlight leech through her thick curtains. When she finally did awaken, it was to find Mr. and Mrs. Mitchell wandering down into the living room to see where their hostess was.

"Oh, there you are!" exclaimed Diane, flinging her arms wide at the sight of Abigail. She was already wearing full makeup and her hair had been dressed. The sweater and trouser set she wore the evening before had been exchanged for a down vest over a red long-sleeve shirt and a pair of slim-fitting jeans. These were fastened with a wide leather belt and a shiny silver buckle.

"*Gute mariye,* Mr. and Mrs. Mitchell. I'm so sorry that I don't have breakfast ready for you. I seem to have overslept."

"That's quite all right. We're in no hurry." James, who had either awoken much later than his wife or simply wasn't as interested in his appearance, was wearing a baggy pair of flannel pajama pants and an oversized t-shirt. His gray hair was sticking up in numerous directions, and he still had lines from his pillow creasing his cheeks.

"I'd be happy to help, if you'd like," Diane offered. "I don't cook much, but I can make a decent quiche."

"No, no. I appreciate it, though." A sense of panic settled inside Abigail's chest at the idea of her guests having to do anything like that for themselves. She prided herself on running a cozy and efficient bed and breakfast, and it simply wouldn't do if word got around that she was slacking off. Nobody would really blame her after everything that had happened, but that wasn't the point.

She dashed off to the kitchen to start a pot of coffee and begin breakfast. She usually had her meals planned out for the week, and today was no exception. All the ingredients she needed for potato pancakes were ready and waiting for her.

Just as she finished shredding the potatoes, she heard heavy footfalls on the stairs. Jacob was awake; hopefully he and the Mitchells would be able to provide decent company for each other until breakfast was ready. She began mixing the eggs and flour into the shredded potatoes.

But Mr. Sutter was not interested in socializing, nor in sticking around for breakfast. He stormed into the kitchen fully dressed and with a sour look on his face. "I'm checking out. What do I owe you?"

Abigail stared at him, wooden spoon in hand and her mouth open in astonishment. "What do you mean? Have you looked outside?" She gestured at the window behind her.

"No. But it's time for me to go." He made no move to check

the road conditions. "I came to find Daniel, and I did. There's no reason for me to stay."

Abigail set the spoon down and crossed the kitchen to where Jacob stood in the doorway. "I know that things have been tough with the death of your friend, but you really can't leave right now. You'll never get anywhere in snow this deep, and even if you do you'll freeze. You're welcome to stay until the weather clears. Don't worry about the room charge."

Her kindness did not sit well with Mr. Sutter. He whipped several bills out of his pocket and slammed them onto the counter. "I don't need your charity, Ms. Lapp. I can pay for as many rooms as I need to. And I can also leave whenever I want to. In case you have forgotten, I have a horse, not a vehicle." He turned on his heel and stomped off.

There was nothing Abigail could do to stop him, and so she let him go. She didn't like the idea of him trying to travel just now, but he was determined. She could only pray for the safety of both him and his horse. The innkeeper barely glanced at the money as she picked it up off the counter and stuffed it into the pocket of her apron. She could tell right away that it was too much. Since the man hadn't given her a chance to tell him how much the fee for the room actually was, she made a mental note to forward the extra cash on to a family in need for the holiday season.

Soon enough, the mouth-watering scent of the pancakes had filled the kitchen and drifted out into the living room. The Mitchells came in, hopeful that breakfast was ready for them.

"That smells amazing!" Diane raved. "I wish I could hire you to come and cook for us all the time. Of course, I think it would all go straight to my hips, but I'm not sure I would care."

James seated himself and inhaled deeply. "Maybe you should just learn to cook for yourself, Diane. Then we wouldn't have to wait until we take these long road trips to have a good meal."

His wife slapped him playfully on the arm, and the two of them dug in. Abigail served the potato pancakes with a topping of sour cream—fresh from the farm, of course—and green onions. She had also cooked up sausage patties and scrambled eggs to go with them.

The two guests were so busy enjoying their meal that it took several minutes before they could clear their mouths enough to say anything else. "By the way, where was Mr. Sutter off to in such a hurry? I tried to ask him, but he was too involved with getting out the door to reply. I hope there wasn't some emergency."

Abigail dug the side of her fork into her pancakes. She had wondered the same thing, but there had been no way for anyone to get a message to their erstwhile guest. He hadn't left the building to use the phone, and nobody had come calling. "Not that I'm aware of. He simply said it was time for him to leave."

"In this weather?" Mrs. Mitchell protested. "That's insane. I know the Amish are much tougher than we are, but he's going to get himself killed."

The innkeeper lifted her shoulders and let them drop. "I agree. But I think he was just too upset about his friend. He hasn't exactly had a good experience here because of all that. He said that he had found Daniel, and it was time to move on."

"Where was he from?" James inquired. "I never thought to ask."

Abigail tilted her head to the side as she slowly chewed a bite of sausage. "You know, I don't think he ever told me. Mr. Sutter seemed to be a very private man, though."

Mr. Mitchell seemed to accept this and polished off his meal.

Amos came through the back door a few minutes later. He was bearing his customary armload of chopped firewood, only this time it was covered in white snow. Before he closed the door behind him, Abigail noticed the wall of snow two feet high that had come to rest in the doorway. It was likely even deeper out on the roads and fields where it wasn't sheltered by an overhang.

"I still have plenty of leftovers from breakfast if you're interested," Abigail suggested. "I think it's still warm, too."

Her nephew bent over to stack the pieces of wood close to the stove so they would dry. "I would love to, but I need to go help Mr. Sutter."

Abigail didn't miss the look that the Mitchells exchanged, but she purposely disregarded it and kept her focus on Amos instead. "Mr. Sutter left almost an hour ago."

But the young man shook his head, fighting off a smile. "He might have tried, but I'm afraid he hasn't made it off the property yet. Look." Amos led her to the kitchen window and pointed at the barn. Jacob was only just then finishing up the task of hitching the horse to the buggy. The beast stood patiently, but it was plain to see by the man's actions that he was frustrated. He clumped back and forth in the shallower snow under the open-sided shed, flinging his hands in the air and shaking his head. At one point, he stepped too far backwards and tripped right into the snow bank.

Abigail pressed her hand against her lips to keep from laughing. "He's upset. I'm sure that if he wasn't dealing with the death of his friend as well as the snow, he would have been long gone by now." She faced Amos once again. "And it's very kind of you to help him. You go ahead, and I'll prepare a jug of hot cider you can take to him when he's finally ready to leave."

It was difficult not to watch out the window constantly as Amos made his efforts to help Mr. Sutter. The Mitchells were curious as well, never having hitched up a horse and buggy themselves and particularly not in the snow. They were more blatant about observing the task, standing at the back door and casually sipping herbal tea while Abigail moved about behind them. She cleaned the dishes, wiped down the table and the counters, and began preparing for lunch, all the while stealing peeks and glances through the curtains.

Amos, with his long legs and farmer's stride, made his way easily through the snow to Jacob and his buggy. The other man stopped and glared at him for just a moment, most likely as Amos was explaining that he would help, before he threw his hands in the air and gestured for the young man to step up and do the work. Amos readily did so, making the task look easy. In only a couple of minutes, the conveyance was ready to go.

Abigail made herself busy with tending the kitchen, but she did look back out the window in time to see Jacob take his place on top of the buggy and slap the reins. The horse obediently stepped forward. The buggy rolled along behind him for a few yards, but once it got into the deep snow it would go no further. Jacob yelled and slapped the reins again, and the horse tried harder, but still the carriage refused to budge.

Amos was at the side of it again, apparently trying to explain something to Jacob. The older man shook his head and made faces, but finally nodded his head and assisted Amos in putting both the horse and the buggy back in their rightful places for the moment.

Abigail had the promised jug of cider ready when the guest returned to the house. Even though Jacob would no longer be traveling today, she offered him a mug of the steaming drink the moment he came through the door.

"No!" he barked as he stripped off his coat and hat. "No, thank you." He stalked back upstairs without any explanations. The Mitchells giggled in the kitchen.

CHAPTER EIGHT

I t was nearly lunchtime when Amos finally returned to the bed and breakfast. Once he had put Jacob's horse and buggy up, he had been occupied with his other farm chores. The Mitchells were reading in the living room, and Jacob had yet to come back down stairs. Abigail pulled her nephew into the far corner of the kitchen by the pantry for a word.

"I think Mr. Stutter is acting rather oddly," she began. "He never should have tried to leave today. Any reasonable person would know that."

The young man bobbed his head in agreement. "He didn't seem like he wanted me to help him at first. In fact, he looked angry that I was even out there. I guess he realized that he would never get it done himself if he didn't accept some assistance. Even so, it irritated him that I could get it done so quickly. It wasn't until the horse was unable to pull the buggy that he finally admitted defeat. *Ant* Abigail, I've never heard so many curse words come out of an Amish man's mouth."

While her other guests seemed to find Jacob's plight amusing, Abigail found this exchange rather disturbing. "It seems to me that he should have been able to hitch up the buggy just fine on his own. I tried to justify his actions with his grief, but now I'm not so sure."

"He's a grown man," Amos agreed. "It's the sort of thing he would have learned a long time ago."

Abigail tapped her lip with a finger. "Did he say anything else to you? Anything about why he wanted to leave so badly or where he was going?"

Amos crossed his arms in front of his chest and studied his boots as he thought. "I don't think so. He was just really ready to leave and was very angry that he couldn't. I felt sorry for his horse."

"I don't have any substantial reason to say so, but I think we need to keep an eye on him," Abigail said. "I'm sure it's nothing, but the deputy confirmed that Mr. Bradford's death was a homicide. He told me to be careful."

Her nephew's mouth was a straight line, and his eyes were squinted in concern. "I told my father that I would be back to help fix the barn. One of the *kieh* kicked through the siding and all the snow is blowing in. But I can get someone else to help him so that I can stay here with you."

Abigail laid a hand on her nephew's arm. "I thank you for your concern, Amos. Really I do. But I'll be fine. Whatever might be happening, I don't think it has anything to do with me. You go ahead and take care of the cattle."

Amos gave her a doubtful look. "I don't like it. You shouldn't be here alone. Maybe someone else could come and stay with you..."

"No," Abigail insisted. "If there *is* something fishy going on around here, then it will only make him more suspicious of us. I think that would be the exact opposite of what we want. And I'm not here alone. The Mitchells are still here."

The young man rolled his eyes. "No offense to them—they seem like nice enough people—but I have my doubts as to how well they might be able to protect you should something happen."

Abigail reached into the pocket of her apron. "I'll be all right. I promise. Here, I owe you some money for all the work you've done around here." She pulled out the stack of bills that Jacob had left on the counter earlier and began counting some of them out.

"I've told you before that you don't have to do that. I'm happy to help you out without pay. You're family, and it's the right thing to do."

She had heard this argument many times before, but Abigail felt that it was the right thing to do. He needed a little bit of money for running around and enjoying himself. But she wasn't worried at the moment about whether or not he wanted any wages. There was something else that had taken over her mind.

"Do these look strange to you?" The notes in her hand were too thin, too smooth. She handed one of them to Amos. "I'm not an expert, but I don't think they're quite right. Of course, they could just be old."

Amos held one up to the light. "I think you're right. Where did you get these?"

Abigail pressed her lips together. If she told him, then he would only be that much more insistent about staying. "I'll have to figure that out. I'll get your money to you later." She would have to take them to the bank to see what they thought and what to do with them.

"You know you don't have to worry about it." He bent down and picked up a crumpled piece of paper from the floor. "I think you dropped this."

Taking the scrap, Abigail unfolded it. It had been torn out of a small notebook, and from the numerous folds across she could tell it had been opened and refolded numerous times. Several numbers were written on it in pencil. She could tell by the way the figures were formed that they had been jotted down hastily. She held it out toward her nephew. "I don't know what this is."

He took it from her and frowned as he looked it over. "I can't say for sure, but my guess would be bank account numbers. Where did it come from?"

Abigail racked her brain, trying to work it all out. She had to find a way to get the pieces of the puzzle to fit together, and that wasn't going to happen while standing around in the kitchen. "I have some things to figure out. You go ahead and do your work in the barn, but I might have need of you later."

Amos came to stand squarely in front of his aunt. "You're worrying me, *Ant* Abigail. There's something going on here, and you aren't telling me all of it."

"You're a smart boy, Amos," she replied, returning his gaze. "But there are some things that just can't be said out loud, not until I know for sure. I promise you that I'll have need of you later; I think I'll need to call Deputy Tynes and ask him to come over for a chat soon."

Clapping his hat on his head, Amos bolted for the back door. "I'll do it right now."

"No, Amos. It isn't time yet. I have to figure some things out before I talk to the deputy. There's no point in having him come here too soon." She glared at him where he stood by the back door, waiting for him to argue with her.

His shoulders sagged and he nodded. "Okay. But I'll be back to check on you later."

Abigail watched as her nephew left, lifting his feet high as he made his way across the field to the barn. She couldn't see the hole in the barn wall from here; it must have been on the other side.

With the broth for the dumplings not yet boiling, Abigail sat down at the table with a cup of tea to think. She let the steam fill her nostrils as she once again ran through everything that had happened over the last few days. Chaser paced back and forth underneath her chair. He rubbed his cheeks on the legs of the seat, waiting for attention, but he also paused every few turns as though he was listening for something.

"I know," she whispered to him. "Something is just wrong. You know it, I know it, Amos knows it, and even Deputy Tynes knows it. But I don't think any of us quite knows exactly what it is."

With a wrinkled brow, the innkeeper studied once again one of the bills that Jacob had given her. It was most certainly not a regular bank note. Was Jacob a counterfeiter? Did he believe that she was too naïve to realize that it wasn't real money? She hadn't ever met a Plain person who would contemplate doing such a thing, but that didn't mean it was out of the realm of possibilities.

What if he wasn't making fake bills, but they had been given to him by someone else? Just because Abigail was able to spot the difference didn't mean that Jacob would be able to. She could be casting blame on him for something that he was completely oblivious to. That didn't seem fair.

In the midst of all this, she had to wonder if she was looking in the wrong direction. The Mitchells arrived at the Troyer Farms Bed and Breakfast first, meaning they were probably in closer proximity to the inn when Daniel had passed away. They seemed like nice enough folks, but they were also *Englisch* like Daniel was. That didn't mean that they had killed him, but if she was smart she wouldn't completely eliminate the possibility. Diane had seemed to overreact when she heard about Mr. Bradford's death, and James hadn't wanted her to talk about it at all. She could have a pair of killers sitting right in the next room.

She brought out the scrap of paper with the numbers on it from her apron pocket and set it on the table in front of her. The tea went cold as she contemplated what these numbers could mean. If they were bank account numbers, then they could be very significant. Abigail and the other folks she knew in the Amish community were not greedy people, but she did understand what money and finances often did to other individuals.

Even though Amos had asked her, Abigail had been reluctant to tell him where the slip of paper had come from. She knew full well that it had come from Mr. Bradford, falling out of his pocket when the paramedics nearly dropped him. The rest of the day had kept her busy enough that she had completely forgotten about it. But she knew that Amos was already up in arms over the whole affair, and she didn't need the young man to go shooting from the hip because he felt overprotective of his aunt.

Abigail turned the piece of paper over and over in her hand, wondering what the numbers meant. Amos could very well have been right about them being bank account numbers. If that was true, then it didn't really lead her anywhere. Daniel Bradford could simply have been a forgetful man who needed to have his notes with him when he went to the bank. It could also have been something much more complicated and sinister than that. She had no way of knowing for sure—nothing more than a hunch, but the combination of the bank account numbers and the potentially counterfeit money made her think she was on the right track.

The innkeeper took a deep breath and puffed it out through her cheeks. She always did her best to be kind and courteous and to take care of her customers in the best way possible. Even if they were rude or unappreciative, she always turned the other cheek instead of confronting them. It was a nice way of living most of the time, but she had the evidence in front of her that said it was time for her to take action. It was time for her to be a little bolder.

Rising from the chair, Abigail slipped the odd-looking bank note back into the pocket of her apron. She took the piece of paper from the table and laid it on the edge of the counter, unfolded and available for anyone to see. If it really did mean anything, she would find out soon enough. Next, Abigail went back to the stove to finish lunch. The broth was boiling.

CHAPTER NINE

"**L**unch is ready whenever you are!" Abigail called into the living room thirty minutes later, ensuring that her voice carried up the stairs as well. The chicken and dumplings were hot and steamy on the stove, ready for her guests to enjoy. Chaser sat patiently next to the stove, hopeful that a random tidbit or two might fall to the floor.

The Mitchells quickly filed into the room. "Abigail, you've got us spoiled on bed and breakfasts from now on," James raved as he took his seat at the table. "We've never been treated so well."

"And we're spoiled on restaurants, too," Diane added. "And don't think we haven't noticed that you've gone above and beyond the services you normally give. We plan to compensate you for all this extra food you've had to dish out."

Abigail pasted a smile on her face, but it didn't match the galloping rhythm of her heart. "I appreciate your kind words, but I don't want you to feel obligated to do such a thing. It's true that I wouldn't normally cook so much for my guests, but special circumstances call for special actions."

Mrs. Mitchell served herself a generous ladleful of the dumplings and inhaled deeply. "Special actions, indeed! But we will most definitely be adding some extra on to the bill. Jim and I have already discussed it. We have plenty of money in our travel fund, don't we honey?"

James scowled at his wife. "Don't brag, dear. It isn't polite."

She scowled back. "Oh, you. Always reprimanding me. If you didn't like my mouth, then you shouldn't have married me. You've always known I couldn't control it." She leaned over her bowl and inhaled deeply. "You should open a restaurant, Abigail."

Silently, the innkeeper agreed with her. Having a restaurant meant she wouldn't have to deal with guests dying in her rooms, murder mysteries, and strange men who only caused trouble. But it also meant that she would be stuck in the kitchen, unable to see her guests enjoy the food she had cooked for them. "I'll keep that in mind," she promised.

"You be sure to let us know if you do it," Mr. Mitchell said. "We'll tell everyone we know, and we know a lot of people. As a matter of fact, I plan on telling plenty of people about your little B&B here when we get back to Indiana after the holidays."

"Thank you." Abigail sat down at the table in front of her plate, but she was too busy thinking to concentrate on her meal. Judging by the way Mrs. Mitchell dressed, how she talked about her job, and the way she bragged about their travel account, the two of them had plenty of money. Did the bank accounts have anything to do with them? Did Mr.

Bradford know something about their finances that he shouldn't have? True, neither James nor Diane had given any regard to the scrap of paper, but they might not have seen it. They could be blissfully inattentive when it served them to be.

Heavy footsteps sounded on the stairs, and Jacob Sutter soon appeared in the kitchen doorway. Abigail's heart pounded even harder. "Please do come in and have lunch with us."

He hesitated for a moment, examining the table with the smiling faces around it before entering. He only took a few steps before stopping again. "What's this?"

The innkeeper turned around to see that he had stopped by the edge of the counter. His finger was pointing at the note, and his grim face looked pale and angry. "Oh, I found that yesterday. Is it yours?"

Jacob snatched the paper off the counter and advanced on Abigail. "This is Daniel's handwriting. I'd recognize it anywhere. Where did you get it?"

She fought hard to keep calm. Her insides were shaking so hard they could start an earthquake, and she folded her hands primly in her lap to keep it from showing. She wanted to run away, to cower in the corner, or even to scream, but she knew she had to be brave. "I think it fell out of Mr. Bradford's pocket. Do you know what it is?" She blinked innocently up at the tall man.

"I think you know perfectly well what it is," he growled as he came closer.

Abigail stood. Jacob was getting too close for comfort. "Perhaps you can explain it better, but I'm fairly certain it has something to do with those fake bills you gave me yesterday.

Mr. Bradford would probably be happy to explain if he were still around." She was vaguely aware of Chaser, who had left his spot by the stove and was now striding back and forth behind his mistress, a deep growl emanating from his throat.

Her challenge only made Mr. Sutter's rage grow. His face turned red, then purple. "What did he tell you?"

Abigail merely shrugged.

Jacob lurched forward, snatching at Abigail's arm in fury. "I don't have time to devise a nice tidy death for you like I did for Daniel. But don't think I'm going to let you put me in jail just because you put on the act of an innocent Amish woman." He suddenly seemed aware of the fact that Mr. and Mrs. Mitchell were watching the scene unfold in front of them. "And the same goes for the two of you! Just listening to you bicker with each other for the last day is enough to make me want to get rid of you."

His fingers closed around the top of Abigail's arm. Chaser leapt up from the floor and launched himself at the assailant's face. Jacob let go of the innkeeper to flail and bat at the creature on his face, but Chaser was not so easily deterred. His paws were a blur of color as he went to work, his ears pinned against the back of his head. He spat and snarled as he continued his attack.

Mr. Sutter stumbled backwards and tripped over Abigail's dining chair. Both he and the piece of furniture fell to the floor with a heavy thud. The impact was enough to scare Chaser off. The cat bolted from the room like a bullet, something furry clasped in his jaws.

Abigail stood frozen as she looked down at her would-be attacker. The feline had done a good job, leaving long red scratches crisscrossing the man's cheeks. Bright drops of blood welled up out of several of them. Normally, if a person had been injured on her watch, Abigail would have rushed to his side to tend to his wounds. But she was rendered immobile by the clean-shaven face before her, and how familiar it looked. Jacob was one of the men in the photo that had fallen out of Daniel Bradford's Bible.

Uncertain what to do, Abigail looked to the Mitchells for help. They looked just as stunned as she felt. Mr. Mitchell sat with a forkful of dumpling halfway to his open mouth. Mrs. Mitchell stared down at the upended Jacob with wide eyes and her perfectly manicured hands pressed to her lips. Jacob was getting his arms underneath himself and disentangling his legs from the chair. Abigail knew there was little she could do to overpower the tall man, and it would take her too long to run through the snow to fetch Amos or get to the phone to call for help.

Just as she was beginning to feel desperate, the front door swung open and hit the wall with a bang. Deputy Tynes appeared in the kitchen doorway a moment later, a second officer and Amos immediately behind him. He only looked at the tableau in the kitchen for a moment before springing into action. He stood over the man on the floor. "Lance Bradford, you're under arrest for the murder of Daniel Bradford."

CHAPTER TEN

"I'm sorry, Abigail. I know you asked me not to call the police yet, but I could tell there was much more going on than you were willing to tell me." Amos leaned heavily against the kitchen counter and regarded his aunt with a woeful expression.

She patted him on the arm. "It's quite all right. It turns out I was wrong, anyway. Not about what was going on, but about when to call the police. Maybe I shouldn't have taken it into my own hands like that, but I couldn't stand the thought of pointing the finger at anyone until I knew for certain."

Deputy Tynes was standing by to put in his two cents. "And you very nearly could have gotten yourself killed, too. I warned you to be careful, Ms. Lapp."

Abigail bowed her head. "I know. I'm sorry. But I hope you understand."

"Well, I don't!" Diane exclaimed. She was still seated at the table. The plates of chicken and dumplings had long gone cold, but the Mitchells hadn't moved from their spots as the police dragged the man they had formerly known as Jacob Sutter out to their squad car. "I don't understand a single bit of what has just happened."

Deputy Tynes raised an eyebrow at the guest and then turned to Abigail with a glint in his eye. "You care to explain it to them? I'm interested to hear how you put it all together."

Abigail sat at the table and invited the deputy and Amos to do the same. "It wasn't anything more than intuition and suspicion, I'm afraid. I'm no detective," she admitted.

But Deputy Tynes didn't seem to mind. "Apparently, you don't need to be to put a murderer in jail. Go on," he urged.

"I didn't really know what to think at first. When I was told that Mr. Bradford had been poisoned and his brake lines had been cut, it was just as obvious to me as it was to everyone else that he had been murdered. But I couldn't figure out why. He seemed like such a wonderful man. He was a good man. But of course, some people can't handle having good people around who are determined to do the right thing."

She took a deep breath, trying to remember it all. She felt that if she didn't just let it all fall out of her mouth, she might never quite understand it herself. "Jacob—I mean, Lance—wasn't able to hook up his horse and buggy. He should have been able to do that without a problem, and he also should have known that a horse would never be able to pull him through this awful snow. But it was the money he paid me with, that truly made me wonder about him." She pulled the wad of cash out of her apron pocket and handed it to the police officer.

Deputy Tynes frowned at the bills, holding them up to the light. "Counterfeit, for sure."

"I was afraid of that," Abigail admitted, "but I also thought there might be a chance that they had been given to him by someone else. I've heard of such things happening. Even though I was already feeling uneasy about him, I couldn't possibly jump to that conclusion without hard proof."

"You know, you didn't need to wait," Deputy Tynes cut in. "If you had called me, I would have been glad to help you out. I could have at least checked out the bills to see if they were counterfeit or not."

Abigail shrugged. "I suppose that's true, but I still had one other mystery on my hands. When the paramedics removed Mr. Bradford's body from the house, a piece of paper fell out of his pocket. I completely forgot about it until it fell out of my own pocket. Amos suggested that the numbers were bank accounts. I wasn't sure what the link was to Jacob or his fake money, but I had a feeling that they were important. That's why I laid the paper on the counter. When Jacob—I'm sorry, I mean Lance—found them, he became furious."

"It's a good thing that Amos went ahead and called me," Deputy Tynes said. "I had been doing plenty of investigating of my own. It turns out that Lance Bradford is Daniel Bradford's brother. Lance had made quite a bit of money illegally, and he was storing it in offshore bank accounts. Daniel knew about them and had sent an email to the Internal Revenue Service. Detectives in his home town let us know about it, but we just couldn't figure out where to find Lance."

Abigail leaned forward in her seat. "So the two of them were brothers? I saw the photo of them in Mr. Bradford's belongings, but I didn't quite make the connection. Well, not until Chaser pulled off his fake beard." She turned around to look at the cat, who was now quietly protecting his new toy underneath the stove. Nobody had been able to convince him to let go of the beard since he had ripped it from Lance's face.

"Why did he pose as an Amish man, anyway?" Mr. Mitchell asked. "That doesn't seem like the smartest thing to do when you're coming to Amish country."

"He couldn't very well come as himself, if his brother knew he was after him," Amos volunteered. "Besides, we tend to be trusting. He looked Amish and had an Amish name, so we were willing to go along with it. I didn't start to wonder about him until the buggy incident."

"Oh, this is so exciting!" Diane declared. "Not only did we get to stay in this quaint little Amish village, but there was a murder mystery unfolding right around us! I can't wait to get home and tell all my girlfriends!"

"Diane…"

This time, Mrs. Mitchell was willing to listen to her husband. The harsh look she was getting from Deputy Tynes probably helped to quell her elation. "Sorry," she muttered.

"What I don't understand," Abigail said, "is how Lance both gained access to Mr. Bradford's car to cut his brake lines and replace his heart medicine. If he had been close enough to do those things, then why didn't he just kill him on the spot?" It felt like a harsh question to ask, but she had to know.

"I'm afraid I only know part of that answer," the policeman said. "Daniel's neighbors had witnessed his brother coming over just a day before he left town. My guess is that Daniel told him what he knew, or he did something to make Lance believe that he knew. He must have done those deeds before he left, hoping that the death would look like an accident."

"Still, I suppose he must have known that his brother was after him. That explains why he wanted so badly to get away from the city, and why he didn't stop to ask for help when his car went off the road." Abigail reflected sadly on Mr. Bradford, but she took comfort in the fact that at least his case had been solved.

Mr. Mitchell slapped the tabletop heartily. "It sounds like you have quite the cracking team of detectives, Tynes. I'm used to lazy cops who don't try very hard. Why, I don't think our local police force would know what to do if such a thing happened around there."

Deputy Tynes took the compliment with hesitation. "Thank you, but I hope we don't ever need to look into anything like this again. It's all done now, at least."

"Yes," Abigail concurred. "And just in time for Christmas. I know the roads are still bad for traveling, Mr. and Mrs. Mitchell, and I'd like to invite you to spend the holiday with us. You're welcome to come, too, Deputy Tynes."

There was much nodding and agreeing all around. Abigail once again found that cozy feeling inside her heart, knowing that she would be celebrating the season with family and good friends.

The End

ABOUT PUREREAD

T hank you for reading!

Here at PureRead we aim to serve you, our dear reader, with good, clean Christian stories. You can be assured that any PureRead book you pick up will not only be hugely enjoyable, but free of any objectionable content.

We are deeply thankful to you for choosing our books. Your support means that we can continue to provide stories just like the one you have just read.

PLEASE LEAVE A REVIEW

Please do consider leaving a review for this book on Amazon - something as simple as that can help others just like you discover and enjoy the books we publish, and your reviews are a constant encouragement to our hard working writers.

OUR EXCLUSIVE READERCLUB (FREE TO JOIN)

If you would like to hear about new titles, free books and special offers by our team of talented PureRead authors be sure to sign up and **become part of our Exclusive Reader Club. It's quick, easy and 100% free.**

SIGN UP NOW at PureRead.com/readerclub

FOLLOW PUREREAD ON AMAZON

To follow PureRead on Amazon visit our Amazon Author page and click on the big yellow +**FOLLOW** button - **amazon.com/author/pureread**

LIKE OUR PUREREAD FACEBOOK PAGE

Love Facebook? We do too and PureRead has a very special Facebook page where we keep in touch with readers.

To like and follow PureRead on Facebook go to **Facebook.com/cleanchristianromance**

OUR WEBSITE

To browse all of our PureRead books visit our website at PureRead.com

BOXSET READING ENJOYMENT

ENJOY HOURS OF CLEAN READING WITH SOME OF OUR BESTSELLING BOXSETS...

Search for Pureread Box Sets on Amazon or visit our website at **PureRead.com/boxsets**

** BROWSE ALL OF OUR BOX SETS **
PureRead.com/boxsets

PUREREAD READER CLUB

DON'T FORGET TO SIGN UP FOR UPDATES AND BECOME PART OF OUR EXCLUSIVE READER CLUB

 JOIN THE READER CLUB (IT'S FREE)

TO RECEIVE PUREREAD UPDATES GO TO
PureRead.com/readerclub

20758811R00049

Made in the USA
San Bernardino, CA
29 December 2018